I'm here to help

S F Chapman

Striped
Cat
Press
™
Concord, California USA

I'm here to help
by
S F Chapman
is also available as a
Large Print Paperback
and as a
Kindle e-Book

Publicity for S F Chapman and *I'm here to help*
exclusively by JKS Communications:
Contact Marissa@JKSCommunications.com

The pawing cat logo is a trademark of
Striped Cat Press.

Visit us at Stipedcatpress.com

Striped Cat Press
First Paperback Edition, Fourth Printing:
September 2012

Works by S F Chapman

To my father Dean Chapman,
a great inspiration to me
and a longtime author in his own right.

Acknowledgments
Although the writing of fiction may seem like a solitary undertaking, it really isn't. True, I did spend many hours alone developing the ideas that went into *I'm here to help* and eventually I pecked away in seclusion at the keyboard of my ancient Apple iBook to produce a tangible rendition of the story; but thereafter, I had plenty of help from several great people.

First; I'd like to thank my brother, Mark Chapman, Ph.D. Mark has patiently edited all six of my novels and provided invaluable advice and suggestions to me. I hope that he will allow me to repay him by working with him on his future literary projects.

Second; I'd like to thank my hardworking nephew, Clinton D. Anderson. Clint is the Photographer and Graphics Designer who produced the cover for the book. With no shortage of talent, he was also one of my three editors for this book. *I'm here to help* would never have made it to print without Clint's excellent work.

Lastly; many thanks are due to my teenage daughter, Christina. Tina has helped me greatly with many of my novels, often coming up with the "sound" to match the various personalities in my books or by suggesting interesting names for the casts of characters. Tina is an exceptional writer and I hope that she will share her talent with the rest of us when the time is right.

1

She poked at the scrambled egg curds on her plate and finally succeeded at skewering the last of them with her fork.

"Mom," she said.

Her tan teenage face swiveled up to stare at me.

I've always been struck by the startling beauty of her eyes: The whites with an iridescent pearly glow, the pupils and irises shiny black, and long lashes like fluttering dark brown feathers fanning the orbs.

"Mom," she said again a bit louder, "I was wondering about something."

I felt a surge of adrenaline and the momentary panic that follows it. Whenever my youngest daughter starts a conversation with that phrase, that seemingly innocent but eventually always sinister introduction, I cringe as to what will follow. "What were you wondering about, Renita?"

She smiled with triumph, she had ventured forth with her query and been met with the proper reply. Renita put down her fork. "You know I've been filling out all of those applications....

I'm here to help

It's kind of boring, college applications are pretty much all the same."

Renita often spoke in little bursts, like many seventeen-year-olds, letting the words escape like a flock of wary birds even before the thoughts behind the utterances were fully ready to take flight. "I typed my name and address way too many times.... and I was pretty much just kind of ignoring what I was doing."

She was building up to a confusing crescendo that I just knew would end with a startling conclusion.

"Then I got to this one application, I don't even remember which college it was for but they asked for a copy of my birth certificate."

Renita stopped abruptly, as if the source of the difficulty would be immediately obvious to me.

I dithered at the mention of that particular document.

"Ooohhh..," I said in a protracted exhalation. I felt like a slow moving beast stuck in thick, swampy mud finally seeming to understand the unsettling scrutiny of my second daughter. "It's in the filing cabinet, I think the second drawer."

Her forehead wrinkled and she looked as if she might cry, but even as a baby Renita never really cried; sometimes she'd whimper, in the

2

most extreme agony she would moan in a deep loud tone but she never did cry.

"What is it, dear?" I reluctantly asked her. I certainly did not want to venture back to this long tucked away matter.

"Well, I did find my birth certificate already," some vital thought seemed still struggling to get out, "and I read it. I mean, I really read it for the first time."

I smiled halfheartedly.

She looked down at the remaining bits of food left on her plate. "I don't...I mean, I can't figure out...." She seemed about to give up on her inquiry. "Oh, never mind!"

"No, tell me," I said in the most maternal voice that I could draw up, trying hard to convince her and myself that I really wanted to hear about this dark and menacing problem.

"It just doesn't make sense." Renita looked up again, "The birth certificate says that you're my mom and Dad was my dad."

I nodded, no great mystery so far.

"But there's all this other stuff that I can't figure out. There's just too many details about me."

"Like what?"

"Well, for one thing; if I was adopted, how come the birth certificate says that I was born at home and not in a hospital somewhere?"

She huffed as if she had finally revealed a great and long suppressed secret.

And indeed she had.

2

Disaster seems to always strike me in the morning: the harsh new light of the day in its infancy, the cold stern air, the false cheeriness of the morning. I have always been one who must brood over the morning like a beast over prey.

One must mourn the morning.

The old stove clock ticked resolutely. *Wouldn't It Be Nice* softly played on the tinny AM radio in the back bedroom. Cars sporadically traversed the still sleepy surrounding streets. I must have sat still for far too long.

"Mom...Mom?" Renita looked concerned.

As I pondered how to respond, it finally became clear to me that this had been a collection of tiny, innocent decisions that had stretched out over many months that had all seemed so right at the time but had instead precipitated a profound and unpredictable outcome.

"OK, you're right. I don't know whether I really forgot to tell you about this or if I tried to blot it all out."

I stood up and pushed the wooden chair in to sit tidily beneath the table. "Come with me."

I'm here to help

The living room in our house is small. The walls have always been painted white. The oak plank floor is a darkish brown. The boards groan or chirp to me in a familiar and reassuring way when I walk across them, like a house song. Light from the several vast windows overpowers the room, warming great moving squares on the floor and the furniture. This is the only room in the ancient house that seems friendly and comfortable to me in the morning.

Renita dropped onto the sofa; her sofa she's always called it. Her older sister Katie had long ago claimed the larger one.

I looked around the room. There were dozens of photographs housed in mismatched frames on every surface, vertical and horizontal. They were frozen memories; some happy, many sad and some a bit mysterious. These photos would be my props in the impending tale.

There was a certain one, not very large, with a thin black wooden frame that hung inconspicuously near the hallway door. Others, I'm sure, barely noticed it as they passed by but I've always glanced at it with every encounter, assuring myself of its presence, its loss would certainly be unforgivable. It was *just* a family portrait, just our family. It must have been about eighteen years ago; merely Katie, Jack and I. Renita wouldn't come along for a while. We stood in front of the cottage at that little resort that we stayed at in Mexico. My hair was much longer. Katie was not quite four. And Jack...

We were all smiling, perhaps even aping a bit for the camera, but it was the only near perfect picture that I had of us: husband, wife and child. The child has since become an adult and moved away. The wife is now much older, grayer and less carefree. And the husband had long ago died a sudden and dreadful death. All that was left of that far-off fairy tale was this one photo.

"It started here," I turned and offered the picture to Renita.

She carefully studied the familiar old image.

There are very few truly seminal moments in life and no one seems to recognize them as such while they swirl fleetingly around before being forever consigned to the past. It's only later when the subtle complexities and subordinate clauses fully play out that the momentousness of that long departed juncture become obvious.

This silly little snapshot of an ordinary family vacation long ago was the lone tangible witness to just such an instant.

Renita tapped a long fingernail several times on the thin glass that encased the ancient photo before fidgetingly sweeping the dust from the top edge of the frame.

I'm here to help

"It was our fifth wedding anniversary, really the first that we had any money, Jack and I decided to make up for our crummy honeymoon."

She tilted her head, "What happened on your honeymoon?"

"Oh it was dreadful! Uncle Bill and Aunt Deloris gave us a week at their cabin by the lake as a wedding gift. The thought was nice and it could have been wonderful; but the weather was hot and rainy and Jack and I took turns suffering through the flu." I shook my head in disdain, "We just couldn't wait to go home."

I pointed to the smiling image of Katie in the old photo, "A year later on our first Anniversary I was eight and a half months pregnant with your sister. We were definitely not going anywhere then. For years afterwards we struggled as first-time parents with a demanding toddler."

I smiled at the memory of the protracted misery of the past. I didn't realize it at the time but those were the best years of my life.

"Somebody at the Station told Jack about this funky out-of-the-way resort in Mexico with these cute little cottages and he made the plans for the trip. It was just going to be the two of us for four days."

Renita frowned, "Why is Katie in the picture?"
8

"Aunt Deloris was supposed to look after her but she broke her hip about a week before, we almost canceled the whole thing."

"What happened?"

"Jack decided that we should just take Katie with us and work something out when we got there."

3

Renita handed the frame back to me and I returned it to the spindly nail that had held it in place for so many years.

"We drove for nearly a day in that huge old sedan that we had when you were little."

She giggled, "The boat car?"

"Yeah, that's the one. It was embarrassingly large to drive around town but it sure was comfortable on a long road trip. That was considerably before seat belt laws, so Jack built a little nest for Katie on the back seat with pillows and blankets and she ended up sleeping for almost the entire trip."

I smiled fleetingly, "It was really rather romantic. I was pressed adoringly against Jack on the giant bench seat as he drove the monstrous air conditioned road machine through the farms and ranch land of the Central Valley."

"We arrived late at night," I pointed perfunctorily towards the photo. "For several days we played around at the resort. There was a roughhewn swimming pool with a rock lining that your sister just loved. And, come to think of it, the last time that I rode a horse was at the

10

stables that were just down the road from our cottage."

Renita briefly frowned at my dallying tale, "Where is this all going Mom?"

"Sorry, dear. As lovely as parts of the vacation were, it just wasn't very romantic with an often challenging toddler in tow."

Renita nodded slowly, she seemed to finally picture the situation that we had faced in a detached and adult-like way.

"I'm afraid your sister was a rather fussy and insistent little one. Nearly everything that we did at the resort centered around her. We couldn't go to the local restaurants because Katie would get restless and disrupt the other patrons' meals. We couldn't stay up late or enjoy any sensual pleasures because Katie would wake up and pester us for the rest of the night. We couldn't even go for a walk without having it degenerate into a pathetic little cryingfest."

Renita chuckled as she imagined her contentious older sister spoiling the carefully made plans of others.

"After the second day, I discovered that the resort had a small group of baby sitters on the staff for just those sorts of family emergencies. While Jack watched over Katie as she napped in the afternoon, I went down to the Check-In and tried to arrange for an evening sitter."

Renita's eyebrows arched up hopefully.

"No luck." I shook my head. "All of the 'approved' sitters had been booked up long ago. Apparently most guests signed up for the service when they made reservations months earlier. I recall that the less-than-helpful clerk idly mentioned that they rarely had a cancellation and that I should check back later."

I cringed as I recalled my growing frustration, "We had just two days left. Katie had gotten bored and was especially cranky the next day, precluding any chance of Jack and I having a good time. I trotted down to the Lobby at some point but no sitters were available."

Renita had the sour sympathetic look of someone who's own plans had occasionally been spoiled by an arbitrary situation beyond her control.

"By the late afternoon of our last day, I'd given up."

"That's too bad," Renita sighed.

"I had just thumbed through the Room Service menu and ordered a dinner for us; it's strange because it seems so clear right now even though it was so long ago."

"What?"

"Just as I hung up the phone there was a knock on the door. For some reason I was convinced that it was the world's fastest Room Service with our food."

We laughed together at the thought.

4

Our old gray cat padded silently into the living room.

"I remember that Katie was pressed up next to me when I opened the door, hoping to get a good look at whoever it was that had stopped by."

"It was a young woman; she bowed a little as she waited at the door. She certainly wasn't delivering food but she might have been one of the resort's baby-sitters. Your sister stared at her in awe but I was a bit dismayed that she looked so young and unkempt."

Renita tipped her head in anticipation.

"Finally the visitor spoke, '*Ah, Perdóneme Señora, estoy aquí para ayudarle.*' I remember that she looked hopefully into the room while I painstakingly used my imperfect high school Spanish to decode what she'd said."

I chuckled as I recounted my faltering efforts as a translator, "So *Perdóneme* was easy, it means pretty much what it sounds like: Pardon me. *Señora* is Mrs., I think nearly everyone knows that one. *Estoy aquí*, that would take considerably more effort to figure out. I was pretty sure that *estoy* was the 'first person

14

singular' for *estar* which I seemed to remember meant 'to be.' So *estoy* was probably 'I am.' But 'I am' what? For several seconds, I confused *agua* with *aquí*. Which would mean that our visitor was water? That didn't seem right."

Renita burst into laughter.

"If she wasn't water, what was she? She was here, that made more sense I decided. *Para* meant for, so she was here for something. What could it be? I was going to have to pick apart the word *ayudarle*. I remembered that *le* was a pronoun that was sometimes added to a verb, and *ayudar* seemed to be a verb. 'To damage?' No, that was *averiar*. 'To refrain from eating?' Also unlikely. 'To help?' That had to be it."

Renita was beside herself with glee at my protracted linguistic folly.

"When I put my wobbly translation together, it came out as, 'I am here to help.' That must to be it. She *had* to be a baby-sitter who was sent to look after Katie."

Renita's head bobbed in agreement, she too had struggled with high school Spanish.

"I was more or less sure that I had figured out what she'd said, 'So you're here to help?' I asked her. She nodded and smiled hopefully.

I'm here to help

"Apparently our luck had finally improved. Katie took her hand and led her into the front room of our cottage and I scampered off to the bedroom to tell Jack that we had a sitter."

The cat leapt up on the sofa with Renita and she idly stroked his cheek.

"Within twenty minutes I was dressed and ready to leave, Jack was still finishing up a long shower."

"It was so cute," I smiled at the cheery memory, "Katie and the sitter had constructed a little castle out of sofa cushions and blankets. They were both playing inside with a few stuffed animals. But I realized that I didn't know the sitter's name so I called Katie out of her palace to ask her."

"Your sister was almost four then, very precocious and sometimes a little too big for her own boots. When I asked, 'What's your new friend's name?' she huffed and said, 'Wholeeonaha' really fast."

"What?" Renita wondered.

"That's what I said. 'A little slower,' I pleaded. Katie groaned with displeasure because, of course, I was cutting into her playtime with someone far more interesting than her boring old mom. 'Whooo...Leeee...Onnn...Ahhha,' she repeated before dashing off."

"I said it to myself several times before I finally got it, it was the Spanish pronunciation of Juliana."

Renita had a far-off look of uneasy realization.

"Jack was finally ready. Just as we opened the door to leave, a smartly dressed bellboy arrived with the dinner that I had ordered. I was a little embarrassed that I hadn't canceled all of the extra food but I figured that Katie and the sitter could pick through whatever they wanted while Jack and I enjoyed our dinner date."

I was transfixed by the memory for several seconds.

"What are you thinking about, Mom?"

"What happened next was rather odd. The busboy brought in the food and Jack paid him off. Katie and the sitter peered out of the castle and the busboy said something to Juliana."

"What did he say?"

"I don't know," I shook my head in dismay. "It was in Spanish and it sounded contemptuous and derogatory."

I stared at Renita, "At the time I thought he was unhappy about the furniture being turned into a playhouse, but now I think that he must have especially disliked the young woman for some reason."

I shrugged, "Then Jack and I left for the restaurant."

"In retrospect," I confessed, "I assumed far too much about the young woman who had appeared at our cottage door."

5

"Mom," Renita pulled herself up from the sofa, "all of this talk about food is making me hungry."

"Again?" I teased, "You just had breakfast a little while ago."

Renita scowled at me.

It *was* nearly lunchtime. "Alright, let's get something to eat. We can come back to this story in a few minutes."

I followed her down the hallway. Just as she had done innumerable times before as she past through the open doorway into the kitchen, Renita jumped up and tagged the top of the opening. There were dozens of faint fingerprints on the door trim attesting to previous successful leaps. Katie had taught her the trick years earlier when she joined the Girl's JV Basketball team in her first year of high school. No amount of pestering on my part at the time could break the habit and I'd finally given up after months of trying.

I pulled two slices of bread out of the loaf and dropped them into the toaster while Renita rummaged around in the pantry cabinet. She finally settled on a can of chicken noodle soup,

I'm here to help

"Now with loopy noodles!" she pointed out, mocking the recent TV ad extolling the virtues of the otherwise unremarkable product.

She dumped the lumpy contents into a pan and set it on the stove. "Why didn't you ever remarry after Dad died?"

As I spread mayonnaise and Dijon mustard on the toast, I considered her question carefully. There was so much that she didn't know about Jack. I laid two slices of cheese, one Swiss and one cheddar, on the splayed out toast and then carefully united the two halves into a whole.

"I did date a little bit."

Renita shook her head, "Why don't I remember that?" She poured the steamy soup into a bowl and cautiously conveyed the hot liquid to the kitchen table.

"Well," I mused, "it was almost impossible to do well with two little girls in the house."

She sampled her soup, "Why not when we were older?"

I sat across from her, "I felt like I would betray him. I know it sounds corny, but Jack was the love of my life. I met him when I worked at the Snack Shack in Washington Park during the summer after I graduated from high school. I must have been your age then. He was on a baseball team that practiced there; one day he waited through a huge line of little kids buying rainbow snow cones to get a small Coke for twenty-five cents."

Renita nodded between spoonfuls of soup.

"When he finally got to the counter, I was sweaty and covered with gooey snow cone syrup."

"I'm sure you were adorable!" Renita laughed.

"He ordered his cola and I got it for him. Then he realized that he'd left his money in the dugout."

"Did he have to go through the line again?"

I took several bites of my sandwich, "No, I felt sorry for him and gave him the drink. I made a big show of pulling a quarter out of my pocket and dropping it into the register. He had a huge smile and said that he'd pay me back the next day. I told him not to worry about it, I'd done the same thing before for a few friends who'd stopped by to see me during the summer."

Renita scooped the last of the loopy noodles out of the bottom of the bowl, "So how did you end up dating?"

A wide nostalgic grin stretched across my face, "The next day he slogged through another line

of kids and ordered another Coke. When I put
his drink on the counter, he dropped two
quarters into my hand. 'Thanks for spotting me
the money yesterday.' I was certainly
impressed; up until that point no one had ever
paid me back. 'Do you want to go somewhere
when you finish up here?' he asked. I agreed
and we did. I saw him almost every day from
then on. Six months later we were engaged."

I popped the last bit of the cheese sandwich into
my mouth, "After he died, I was pretty sure that
I would never find anyone like him again. The
whole process of searching for another mate just
made me sad, all I could think about when I was
with another man was how much he wasn't like
Jack,"

Renita gathered up the dishes and set them into
the sink. "With all of the trouble that I've had
with dating in the last few years, I guess I can
understand why you weren't too happy about
having to go through with all of the ploys and
drama."

She turned to face me, "So, how did your big
night out in Mexico go?"

We ambled back to the living room.

6

Renita flopped onto the sofa; I nudged aside the slumbering cat and joined her.

"The dinner date was wonderful. We'd spotted several restaurants near the resort and we spent a few minutes outside of each one considering the menus and talking to the barkers who seemed be at every establishment."

"Barkers?"

"They are often just one of the waiters or sometimes the host," I smiled. "Usually they'll tell you about the specials and any entertainment that they have at the restaurant. We settled on a huge old night club called 'La Alhambra' that looked like a Moorish palace mainly because it had a continuous floor show, a ballroom and seafood tapas which Jack loved."

Renita casually nodded.

"The food and drinks were excellent but mostly I remember the shows which seemed to change every twenty minutes or so."

"What kind of shows?"

"My favorite was the Flamenco dancers. There were several performers who did the most astonishingly seductive rhythmic interplay that I've ever seen. The two men wore black pants and jackets with silver striping and decorations. Two of the woman had colorful traditional outfits. The third woman wore red and black; she was the temptress and she tried to lure the men away from the other women. Finally in the end, the two virtuous woman drove her away and beguiled the philandering men."

I retrieved a glossy black and white of Jack and I sitting at a small round table clinking half-filled glasses from the wall and handed it to Renita.

Her fingers traced the intricate gold embossing on the lower left corner that assured the viewer that the photo had been taken at 'El restaurante famoso La Alhambra, Baja California, Mexico.'

"While we ate a band played folk songs for a while and a woman put on a show with a half dozen parrots. When we finally finished the huge meal and the three or four servings of wine and mixed drinks we decided to dance in the ballroom."

Renita studied the photo again before handing it back to me, "It looks like you had a great time."

"We did, but finally it came to an end," I rubbed my forehead wearily. "I think it was about 2

AM when we left the night club. I remember that we walked back to the resort parking lot and canoodled in the back seat of our car for an hour or so."

"Really?" Renita stared at me in disbelief.

"It was almost like when we were dating and we'd smooch in the car in front of my parent's house after dancing for half the night."

She seemed to have trouble visualizing her prudish old mom engaged in lustful undertakings.

I tipped my head and smiled, "It was our anniversary after all and we weren't likely to enjoy the same pleasures in the little cottage with our nosy three-year-old in the next bed."

"We eventually tiptoed back into our room. Katie and the sitter were asleep together on one of the beds. Jack woke the sitter and thanked her. He gave her a big tip. She asked if she should come back again the next day. She seemed particularly downcast when Jack told her that we were leaving in the morning. I remember thinking that our vacation would have been so much nicer if we'd discovered this young woman when we first arrived instead of on our last evening."

"We slept too late the next morning. Katie finally woke us up at about 7:30. Jack and I shuffled around in a gray haze from the excess of alcohol. It took forever to pack everything and jam it all back into the car."

"Katie was back to being a difficult three-year-old again, running around and getting into trouble. Jack was unusually edgy. I thought at the time that, like me, it was probably a hangover and the lack of sleep."

"When we drove away, I had a strange dark feeling of apprehension."

Renita studied me quizzically.

I shrugged, "It was nothing that I could put my finger on, just a general sense of dread, I guess. When we made it to the highway, Katie had fallen asleep and I decided that I was suffering through post vacation blues."

"So it was nothing?"

"Well," I vacillated, "sometimes I think these things are self-fulfilling prophecies. When you think there will be a problem in the future, any little abnormality that pops up will convince you that you had predicted the difficulty."

"What happened Mom?"

"About two hours after we left the resort, we reached the border crossing in Tijuana. It was a huge facility that reminded me of a bridge toll plaza and an agricultural inspection station combined. There must have been twenty lanes of traffic waiting to pass through; trucks were honking, a few patrol cars with red flashing lights escorted a dilapidated bus to a covered inspection area for further scrutiny, to one side hundreds of people waited on a fenced-off bridge to walk across the border. It was exciting and scary at the same time."

"I've seen pictures of it on the news, I think," Renita said.

"Finally it was our turn. An inspector waved us forward and Jack unrolled the window. The officer was a big grumpy looking fellow, 'where are you coming from?' he asked. Jack told him the name of the resort. 'What is your destination in the US?' 'Our home in Carlson, California,' Jack said."

I laughed when, after nearly twenty years had passed, I had finally recognized the complex irony of what happened next, "Just before the border inspector let us through, he asked, 'Do you have any fruits, meats; cattle hooves, horns or bones, weapons or explosives of any kind, or citizens of any country other than the United States anywhere in this motor vehicle?' Jack just shook his head and the inspector let us cross the border."

"So all of your worrying was about nothing?"

I'm here to help

"I certainly wouldn't say that; Jack glanced nervously at the rearview mirror as we drove away and said, 'I'm glad that's over.' I realized then that it was more than just the hangover that had made him so edgy. 'What is it, sweetie?' I asked. He sheepishly admitted that he had hidden a big box of illegal firecrackers in the trunk for one of the guys at the Station. At the time I thought it was a silly and juvenile thing to do, but now with all of the dour and overblown Homeland Security crap, I think that I would have strangled him for taking such a stupid chance."

"So," Renita frowned at the revelation, "Dad wasn't perfect?"

"I guess most of the time he was, dear."

"It was a long tedious trip home without any of the giddy anticipation of the journey to the resort. We took turns driving. Poor Jack felt miserable after we stopped for lunch, so I drove until dinnertime. We got home just after midnight. I carried Katie in to the house and put her to bed. Jack was just too tired to unpack the car."

"We finally trudged off to bed at about one."

7

I smiled and spread my arms, "We were back here in our uneventful old house. The only part of vacations that I've never cared for is the long slog home after the novelty of the exotic destination. It's just such a let down."

Renita stroked the drowsy cat and the big beast slumberously twisted around to allow a more thorough rubdown.

"As I struggled to fall asleep in my familiar old bed, things just didn't seem to be right. Jack fidgeted and snored, still suffering from the long trip and the lingering hangover. The house creaked and groaned sporadically as if it was expressing its dismay at our recent absence. Down the hallway, Katie now and again cried out in her sleep."

"Eventually, after many hours, I dozed off."

Renita tugged the sleepy cat onto her lap.

"It was dark and cold when I woke up. Our bedroom door squeaked open and I realized that someone was sneaking into our bedroom."

"Oh my god!" Renita blurted.

"It was just Katie," I laughed.

I'm here to help

Renita sighed with relief.

"She often did it when she was little, I think she convinced you to try it a few times when you were three or four. She was never nearly as stealthy as she imagined. Katie stood at the edge of the bed and pestered me to get up and fix her some breakfast. Even though I was wretchedly groggy and grumpy, I eventually pulled myself out of bed."

The cat decided that he'd had enough attention from Renita and bound off the sofa.

"Katie skipped happily down the hallway, she'd gotten plenty of sleep over the last day and a half. I remember just feeling limp and disoriented while your sister ran excitedly around the house trying to discover if anything had changed during the four days that we'd been gone."

Renita's eyebrows arched up expectantly.

I shook my head, "Nothing had of course; but halfway through cooking up some oatmeal, there was a knock on the front door. Katie started shouting, 'There's somebody here! There's somebody here!' and she pranced to the front door."

"Now this is very odd, I thought to myself, who could it be at 6 AM on a Sunday morning?"

"I smoothed back my straggly hair and cinched up my pink bathrobe. By the time I made it to the foyer, Katie had pulled open the door and there was the baby-sitter from the resort!"

Renita frowned, "How did she get here?"

"I had no idea at the time. Katie was ecstatic. She jumped around like a hyperactive little monkey and shouted, 'Juliana! Juliana!' The poor sitter looked dreadful, ashen and unsteady; I thought for sure that she would vomit."

Renita stared at me in confusion.

"As she stood in the doorway, she picked up two of our suitcases from the porch. For a moment I had this crazy idea that we'd forgotten some luggage at the resort and the young woman had doggedly ventured five hundred miles to return the missing items."

"That would have been so weird!" Renita commented.

"But she hadn't of course. With her three-year-old exuberance, Katie tugged the visitor into the foyer and the woman set the suitcases down on the floor. I glanced out on the porch and all of our luggage was neatly lined-up, waiting to be brought in to the house."

"But didn't you say that Dad was too tired to bring it in?"

I'm here to help

I nodded, "While Katie danced around in glee; the sitter stammered, 'I'm here to help' and stared up hopefully at me. Somehow she had followed us from Mexico and now she seemed to want to insert herself into our lives. The poor thing looked like she was especially ill, I remember that she even dry-heaved a bit. Katie became really concerned that her new friend was in such distress."

Renita's eyes were wide with apprehension, "What did you do?"

"I just shook my head. 'You can't stay here.' Her shoulders slumped and she wobbled unsteadily towards the door."

I considered the strange old memory, "Then fate intervened."

Renita tipped her head.

"Katie ran up and slammed the door shut before the woman could leave. The baby-sitter stumbled around your sister and ended up sitting on the floor. She was obviously very dizzy and sick. I didn't know what to do."

Even now, so many years later, the uncertainty and trepidation of that moment unnerved me.

"Katie was incensed. She insisted that we had to take care of Juliana. 'NO! No Mom!' I remember she shook her little head at me in disgust, 'We have to take care of her!' I just stared at the two of them for a long time. Finally I nodded my head and Katie led the visitor off to bed."

8

"Jack was awakened by all of the noise and he finally got up. I told him what had happened. We peeked into Katie's room and she and the woman were curled up in bed. Our unexpected visitor was already asleep."

"We tried to coax Katie out of the room but she just glared at us and snuggled against her new friend."

"We decided to wait a few hours before we figured out what we'd do."

I bit my lip and paced around the living room as I recalled the consternation that I'd felt that morning.

"The whole day was almost like a dream or an odd foreign film."

"I don't understand, Mom."

"It seemed like it was all in black and white; stark with plenty of forbidding shadows, spliced together into peculiar little glimpses of what was obviously a much longer saga, fragments that were strangely symbolic of the jarring passage of time."

Renita watched me pace.

"That's the way that I remember it, a dozen or so truncated scenes."

"Jack and I sat at the kitchen table halfway through our breakfast. I looked questioningly at him. He just shrugged."

"Later, I recalled the clock ticking. The house was otherwise strangely quiet. Sometimes Katie was in bed with Juliana, sometimes the cat slept there."

"Hours drifted by. Jack silently brought in the rest of the luggage. I looked in on Juliana as she slept. I was perplexed."

"Jack and I read the newspaper in the living room, Katie was curled up on he sofa with us. We silently considered the same questions: What was this all about? Why was she here? How had she found us? Would she ever wake up? What would we do next?"

"Even though this happened long before the current ridiculous uproar about unsanctioned border crossings, she was undoubtedly here without papers."

"We just didn't know what to do."

9

"So you just let her stay here?" Renita asked incredulously.

"Well; she was mildly feverish and managed to vomit every few hours," I nodded halfheartedly, still trying to rationalize some apparently unseemly deed from my past.

Renita's lingering scowl indicated that she would have chosen otherwise.

"Eventually Katie convinced us that we should take care of Juliana at least until she got over whatever it was that was ailing her. At the time, I thought that maybe she just had the flu or food poisoning."

I was still faced with the harsh skepticism of my teenage daughter.

"While Juliana slept in Katie's room," I continued, "we spent quite a bit of time speculating on how and why she had arrived at our door."

I smiled at Renita, hoping to win her over to the point of view that I myself had struggled with many years earlier. "More than once we seriously considered calling the police or sending her off to the County Hospital."

36

"Why didn't you?"

"We almost did, but finally Jack and I realized that your sister was right, here was this poor lost soul who needed our help. I found out much later that her situation was really much more dire than I had imagined at the time."

I pointed sternly at my teenage daughter, "She was much younger than you are now, dear."

Renita thought for a moment about that and softened a bit, "Well; I guess I would be grateful if someone took care of me if I got sick a long way from home."

"Slowly Juliana seemed to battle through the worst of it. By the middle of the afternoon she'd stopped vomiting. Just before Katie's bedtime, your sister managed to get her to drink a little water. At around midnight when I finally went to bed, she didn't seem to be feverish and was finally sleeping soundly. I suspect that Jack checked on her just before he went off to work at four in the morning."

Renita slid her hand over her chin and frowned, "That's right! I remember you and Katie saying that he'd leave the house really early to go to work."

I'm here to help

"Most of the time I wouldn't see him at all in the morning but he'd almost always be home by dinnertime."

I hunted around for the picture that I knew epitomized what I remember happened next.

There, high in the left corner of the smooth white wall, surrounded by nearly a dozen ridiculously formal school photos of Katie, was a modest snapshot in a frilly silver frame.

I reached up and plucked the small image from its place.

"For some reason that next morning I slept really late. I guess it was because Katie didn't sneak into my bedroom to clamor about breakfast. I finally woke up at about nine and just lay there for a while. I remember slowly realizing how quiet it was in the house."

I chuckled, "I had this sudden panic that maybe your sister had picked up whatever Juliana had and that there would be two patients barfing in the next room. But then I noticed the smells."

Renita had an almost comical look of dread. "Smells?" she asked cautiously. "What kind of smells?"

"Nothing bad," I laughed. "It was coffee, toast and bacon."

Her sense of foreboding faded.

"I remember spending an absurd amount of time in that stuporous early morning state of mine trying to fathom how and why I was smelling bacon. I knew we had some in the refrigerator but Jack didn't care for it and Katie didn't know how to cook it. Finally I got up and shuffled into the kitchen."

Renita's earlier look of dread had returned, "Was it a disaster?"

"No, just the opposite. It was unsettlingly tidy. Everything was neat and clean, the only things out of the ordinary were a place set at the table for me and a pot of hot coffee on the stove."

"Where were Katie and Juliana?"

I handed Renita the little photo that I'd been clutching. "I wondered the same thing. I found them in here. Your sister was sitting quietly on the floor of the living room coloring a very elaborate picture of some sort and Juliana was on the sofa softly humming and watching over her as she worked."

Renita examined the snapshot of her sister and Juliana smiling together in the living room, "You took this then?"

"I think it was a few days later."

I'm here to help

I grinned at the unexpected bit of luck that the image represented. "It was the same thing nearly every morning for months afterwards. Katie and Juliana would awaken hours before me and silently prepare breakfast together, then tidy up afterwards. Katie would be clean and dressed when I got up. Juliana would be dutifully watching over your sister and keeping her out of trouble."

I laughed at our sudden good fortune, "Jack and I even got to snuggle a bit on the weekends."

"So Juliana became part of the family then?"

"I guess she did. We still didn't know anything about her. We barely spoke; I assumed at the time that it had something to do with the language differences. But it didn't seem to really matter, Juliana fit neatly into our family. It was almost like there was a void that we didn't even know about that her presence seemed to fill."

Renita handed the picture back to me.

"We had a little family birthday party for Katie a few weeks later when she turned four. I recall that Juliana gave her a rag doll that she'd made from scraps that she'd collected from some old clothes that I'd tossed out."

"I remember that doll! Katie wouldn't let me touch it, although sometimes when she wasn't around, I would play with it anyway."

I glanced at the wall of photos and chose the next one that I would use. "For a little while everything was perfect."

I winced at the impending reopening of the old imperfectly-healed emotional wound.

"Five weeks and four days after Juliana knocked on our door, Jack died."

10

Renita stared unnervingly at me as I returned the little snapshot of Katie and Juliana to the wall.

"Mom, you're shaking."

I studied my trembling hand as I struggled to return the picture to its proper place, even after eighteen years of crying and grieving, of adjustments and adaptations, of downcast depression and eventual uneasy acceptance, the mere thought of Jack's sudden death still greatly affected me.

I managed to hook the frame to the nail without dropping it. "I know."

"I've never told you this story before," I retrieved the proud work portrait of Jack from the wall and handed it to Renita, "mainly because I didn't think that I could do it until now without having a breakdown."

Her forehead furrowed as she glanced up to examine me for any signs of imminent psychosis.

She turned to study the picture of the almost mythical man whom she had never personally known but always undoubtedly thought of as 'Dad.'

42

My still quivering hand trailed lightly over her shoulders and I admired the formal photograph along with her.

Everyone at Fire Station 3 had been given the choice of having their portrait taken in their dress uniforms or their everyday turnouts. Jack had chosen the heavy tan protective gear with the familiar black long brimmed helmet.

He stood sideways and turned a bit towards the viewer with his head slightly back. A confident grin peering out from beneath his thick black mustache. He clutched a long wooden handled axe with both hands. Jack had gone to great lengths to point out to Katie and me that the implement was a lumberjack's axe that the photographer had at the studio, not the more appropriate Firefighter's axe with the pick-shaped point opposite the broad cutting edge.

Renita stared for many minutes at the image, "How did it happen?"

I closed my eyes and whispered, "At about five in the morning someone pounded on our front door. Juliana answered it before I even had a chance to get out of bed. A minute or so later she came into my bedroom and tugged at my hand. 'Sharon, Sharon!' she kept saying. Juliana was really agitated."

"I put on a robe and followed her to the door. Just outside on the porch was a Policeman."

I'm here to help

Tears were welling up in my eyes, "I knew something had gone wrong. Jack had been killed in a car crash on the way to the Station. Somebody had run a red light and broadsided the little sports car that he loved to drive. He was killed instantly."

"It's ironic, really; with all of the dangerous stuff that firemen get stuck doing, that a bad driver who wasn't paying attention on a gloomy morning would claim him."

I stood there limply in our comfortable living room while Renita examined the image of Jack. I could feel the burning in my eyes as tears threatened to spill forth. I took great, slow breaths of air and struggled mightily not to cry. No amount of grieving or pleading would ever bring him back.

Renita stood and returned the frame to the wall for me. As she ventured back to the sofa, she wrapped an arm around my waist and held me for a few minutes.

When I felt that I could continue, I stroked her long brown hair and kissed her forehead.

"Everything was a horrible gray blur for weeks afterwards. I apparently identified his body but I don't remember doing it. The guys at the Station arranged for the funeral and burial, I'm sure I was there but I just don't recall anything."

"I think it was about a week after the accident, a Firefighter's Union Rep came by for a few hours to explain the death benefits and to help with settling the estate. Everything would be taken care of, he said. At one point I remember him asking if the 'Nanny' would stay on and tend to Katie. I just nodded."

Renita stared sympathetically into my eyes, "It must have been terrible, Mom."

I finally nodded, "It was; for about a month I had no idea what was going on. Often I would just cry in bed for hours. Sometimes I would cling to his pajamas or one of his work shirts and smell his lingering odor. I'm sure I ate occasionally but I just don't remember doing it. It was all like a dark never-ending nightmare."

"Sometimes Katie would tiptoe in and get some money out of the cash box that we had in the bottom drawer of the dresser while Juliana looked on nervously from the bedroom door. Later I found out that they would walk down to the market and buy food with the cash when there was nothing left in the kitchen. Juliana would answer the door and the phone only to turn away the curious by telling them that I was napping."

"At some point I came to my senses. For a long time I lay in bed and thought about Jack. It was the first time since his death that I could picture him without crying. I remember smelling some sort of food being cooked and I realized how hungry I was. I could hear Juliana speaking to Katie in Spanish. The two of them sang some cheery little songs together. Things had changed in our household and they had adjusted, I needed to adapt too."

Renita followed the sad story with grim fascination.

"At about four in the afternoon I got up and took a shower. Then I wandered about the kitchen in my bathrobe and finally sat glumly at the breakfast table. I remember watching Katie and Juliana cutting up potatoes for French fries. They both glanced warily at me as if I might collapse or erupt in tears without warning. After maybe twenty minutes of cutting and dicing I finally noticed that Juliana was showing."

Renita tilted her head in confusion.

"She was pregnant."

11

Renita's face was frozen in an odd combination of horror and unwelcome realization. She pressed each of the fingertips of her right hand in turn to her thumb several times as she tallied up the years.

She glared at me when at last she'd realized the long hidden truth. "Juliana was my mother?"

I nodded.

"MOM! Why didn't you tell me this before?"

The old gray cat's head bobbed up at Renita's outburst.

"Well, it's much more complicated than you think."

After hours of story telling I certainly couldn't just end it all with some sort of truncated and trite conclusion, 'And that's how you joined our family, little one. Now toddle off and don't ask anymore troubling questions.' She deserved to know of both the laudable good deeds and the lamentable oversights that had led to her current situation.

Her incensed expression lingered.

I'm here to help

The cat finally decided that imminent danger was unlikely and curled up to resume his nap.

As I recalled Juliana's noticeable belly while she prepared dinner with Katie, I chuckled at my fumbling efforts to communicate with her and not tip-off my perceptive four-year-old daughter.

"I staggered to my feet, which unsettled both Katie and Juliana, and tried unsuccessfully to be as nonchalant as possible. I remember rubbing Juliana's belly, which now seems like a particularly weird thing to do."

Renita's earlier anger was softened a bit by my muddled efforts, "What did she say?"

"It was in Spanish, '¡Aye no, soy una vaca gorda!' In my thick state at the time, it took me quite a while to puzzle out what she had said."

"Oh, I'm such a fat cow?" Renita ventured.

"Something like that; I halfheartedly tried a few other things but it was dawning on me that she had no idea why her belly was suddenly expanding."

I slowly shook my head. "I think that realizing that Juliana might be pregnant shook me out of the funk of self-pity that had consumed me since Jack had died. I had to get on with things or I too would probably perish."

The heavy gloom from revisiting Jack's death still hung over me. I kneaded my fingertips against my forehead in consternation.

"This young woman whom I barely knew had stepped up and taken over for me when I couldn't manage, now I needed to repay that kindness."

Renita seemed to grasp the insight that I had stumbled upon eighteen years earlier. "What did you do?"

"I got dressed."

Renita smiled wryly, "Always a good sign for you."

"For the first time in almost a month I joined the world of the living. As we ate dinner together, I thought about when I was expecting your sister. We certainly would need help. I recalled the old midwife that had delivered Katie; her name was Mrs. Gertrude Wilson. Even though I hadn't seen her since Katie was about two, I still called her occasionally and we exchanged Christmas cards every year."

"That night, while Juliana was bathing your sister, I phoned Mrs. Wilson and told her of my suspicions. Barring a delivery that she was expecting, she agreed to stop by the next day."

I hunted around for another photo and handed it to Renita. She studied the snapshot of the worn and gray old woman slumping slightly forward on an oversized wooden rocking chair.

"That was taken a few months before she passed away, I think she was in her early eighties at the time."

"She looks so unhappy," Renita surveyed the image, "or maybe just really stern."

"I think she was worn out, she had a surprisingly difficult life, as I recall. For years she worked ten hours a day six or seven days a week as a checker at Manny's Market. Finally she met Mr. Wilson when she was in her late thirties and they got married. He made plenty of money and wanted a stay at home wife so she quit her job. Working at the market was tough but she realized later that it was also an important social outlet for her."

"How did she become a midwife?"

"The Wilsons tried for three or four years to have kids. She would get pregnant and scurry happily around to prepare for the impending birth but something would always go wrong after a few months and she would miscarry."
"Oh; that's so sad!"

"She never did have any kids of her own. Eventually she went through menopause and that was that. Most women would have just given up but Mrs. Wilson decided to take
50

everything that she'd learned about pregnancy and child birth and turn it into a second career."

"Even though Mr. Wilson wasn't too happy about it, she went to the Community College for the required classes and was eventually certified. By the time I met her she'd been delivering babies for decades. Mr. Wilson died of a heart attack about ten years after they got married and Mrs. Wilson was alone again. Fortunately by then she was quite busy as a midwife. I think she was almost seventy when she stopped by to check on Juliana."

Renita handed the frame back to me and I returned it to the wall.

"Luckily your sister was napping when Mrs. Wilson stopped by. Having Katie under foot would have been a disaster. Mrs. Wilson had just delivered a baby boy at a home a few blocks away and still had on her medical scrubs. I introduced her to Juliana and I was sure that she thought that Mrs. Wilson was a nurse or maybe even a doctor. Mrs. Wilson took a quick look at Juliana and told me that I had probably guessed right about the possible pregnancy."
"Wasn't it really confusing?" Renita frowned, "I can't imagine how scary this must have been for Juliana."

I laughed, "This is why you call in the pros. Mrs. Wilson telephoned an old Spanish speaking classmate who delivered babies in

Tucson. We ended up having a really complicated three-way conversation that went on for a good thirty minutes."

"What did you find out?"

"It took quite a bit of coaxing to get anything more than a very nervous *Sí* or *No* out of Juliana, but eventually we had some very sketchy answers. More importantly, she reluctantly agreed to let Mrs. Wilson examine her. While the two of them were in my bedroom, I talked to the woman in Tucson and I finally learned a bit more about Juliana."

"Like what?"

"Well; I found out that she had hidden behind the suitcases in the trunk of our car when we left Mexico. She jimmied open the lock when the car was in the driveway and carried the suitcases to the porch. Even though she was quite sick from the terrible ride in the trunk, she waited patiently by the front door until she heard Katie pestering me for breakfast."

"Oh my God, that must have been a horrible trip!"

"That certainly explained why she was so sick afterwards. I found out that she was only fourteen and had runaway from home a few months before she showed up at our door at the resort. She didn't even work there. She saw us struggling with Katie during one of our walks and decided to help out. I suspect now that an opportunity for some food and a brief bit of comfort prompted her to finally knock on our door."

"Did she have a family?"

"Apparently not; there was some mention of an Aunt and Uncle that mistreated her but that was all we could get out of her."

I shook my head, "She wouldn't even tell us her last name."

"But you did find out that she was pregnant, right?" Renita speculated.

"Yes; Mrs. Wilson returned with Juliana who had a downcast look of shame after what was almost certainly her first pelvic exam. Mrs. Wilson had her friend explain the situation to Juliana."

"I tried to follow along with the phone conversation but Juliana was really upset and spoke Spanish way too fast for me to keep up. At one point she just kept saying 'NO, NO, NO!' I found out later that the woman in Tucson had mentioned terminating the pregnancy as an option."

"Well I'm glad that didn't happen."

I'm here to help

"Eventually everything settled down and it was agreed that she would have the baby at our house and Mrs. Wilson and I would help her through it."

"Wait a minute," Renita stared at me with a sudden look of dismay, "so after all of that you still had no idea of how she got pregnant and who was the father?"

I just shook my head, "I'm afraid not."

12

Renita had a most agonized look of defeat.

I stroked her cheek, "What is it, sweetie?"

"I've always known that I was adopted," she turned away, "and until now, I was grateful that you had told me the truth about that from the beginning."

Renita scowled and purposefully slid her caramel brown hand over my blotchy ashen arm, "I know a couple of kids who don't look anything like their parents. They felt really betrayed when they finally figured out what everyone else had guessed long before, that they were adopted; like tall pale redheaded Kimberly Santos and her short Filipino parents."

She stared angrily into my eyes, "You should have told me all of this sooner!"

"I'm sorry, I never meant to keep this from you. It's just that..."

"BUT YOU DID!" she flared.

I had always considered my motives regarding Renita's unconventional inclusion in our family to be virtuous; perhaps a bit furtive and tardy, but virtuous nonetheless. "You've only heard part of the story. Up until now, I don't think that you would have appreciated the complexities...."

"NO! You don't understand! I've never had any idea of who I really was and knowing this would have probably helped." She held an infuriated glare for an uncomfortably long time.

"Really?"

Renita nodded, her enraged expression slowly faded, "You and Katie almost always act the same way when things happen. You both cry at the same sappy movies, yell at the waiters when they mess up your food orders and poke around way too much in other people's business when they'd rather just be left alone."

I winced at her perceptive observations. She was right; as much as I had tried to treat them both as equals, I'd frequently favored Katie's confrontational persona mainly because I understood it. Renita was often just a placid impenetrable mystery to me.

"I feel like such a freak sometimes," she sighed in despair. "I don't know anyone else who's like me."

"You can talk to me about your feelings anytime, dear."

She smirked incredulously. "I don't think that you would understand most of it."

"Try me."

She held up one hand.

I studied the appendage for several seconds before shrugging.

"Left-handed, Mom."

"How could that be a problem?"

"Only someone who is right-handed would ever say that," she groaned. "Almost everything is made for the convenience of righties. One of the reasons that I had so much trouble with those guitar lessons that I took when I was twelve was that the teacher wouldn't let me flip the guitar around or restring it for a lefty."

"You never told me that."

"I *did*," she shook her head emphatically, "you said that I should do it the teacher's way before I tried anything else. And my stupid nose!"

I studied her face. Although by no means small, her nose was thin and straight, fitting nearly perfectly on her slender angular face. "It seems fine to me, Renita."

I'm here to help

"That's not the problem, Mom." She rolled her eyes, "When most people get a bit too warm, little drops of sweat form on their brows."

I nodded.

"That doesn't happen to me."

"Oh, the sweaty nose thing!" It had been that way with Renita since birth, tiny glistening drops would appear, not on her brow, but from the tip to the bridge of her nose. When she was a baby it had been a source of some amusement, but as the years progressed, I took it for granted.

"Yes, the nose thing! No one else I've ever met has to self-consciously dab at their nose whenever the weather heats up."

I sighed at her histrionics, "Left-handedness and a sweaty nose doesn't make you a freak."

"I know Mom, but it's not just that stuff." She slumped against the arm of the sofa. "Sometimes for no good reason, I feel like I just can't go on anymore. I feel like I should just give up."

I studied her in disbelief, "What do you mean?"

"It's like a crushing sense of sadness." She closed her eyes and whispered, "It's really terrible. I feel like all of the color and sound has been drained out of everything around me.
58

People seem like pathetic mannequins shuffling mindlessly around tending to their meaningless tasks. Nothing is real or important."

This was definitely not a minor problem.

Renita drew in long labored breaths as she wrestled her way back to composure.

This sounded like clinical depression, I realized.

I scrutinized the downcast teenager that I'd raised from a baby and realized that it was true, unlike her much more contentious older sister, I had no idea of what was really going on inside of her head.

Katie had always been blustery and vocal about her difficulties and aspirations; always straightforward and rarely very subtle. But Renita was quite different. She seemed to prefer to stoically fight her own battles and silently struggle through her own hardships, occasionally looking merely a bit glum when I was sure that she was dreadfully unhappy about some undesired outcome.

In the weary endurance contest of parenting, the noisy one had been considered the problem child and the introspective one the 'good' kid. Apparently Renita had been suffering through many more crippling miseries than I'd realized.

I'm here to help

Undoubtedly, many years before, Juliana had done the same things.

13

It was the cat that finally broke the long hypnotic spell of unwelcome self-reflection when he leapt up on the sofa and nuzzled Renita.

"Juliana, your *real* Mom," I tentatively added the qualifier for the first time, "said it a long time ago, 'I'm here to help' when you have problems."

Renita sighed and nodded. "I know."

All of the revelations and insights of the last several hours had caused us both to teeter repeatedly between soaring exhilaration and oppressive misery. Rummaging around amongst the trapdoors and treasures of the past was an unsettling and perilous endeavor.

"What do I call you now?" Her eyebrows arched up, "Sharon? Not *really* my Mom? Maybe something else?"

I winced at the suggestions; all seemed to relegate me to second-class status, merely the imperfect substitute who took over for the preferred original. "Mom or Sharon, your choice."

I'm here to help

"I'll try Sharon for a little while." Renita bit her lip, "How was the pregnancy? Did I kick and squirm around?"

We'd apparently veered back to a safer and less intimate topic. "For a long time, other than Juliana's expanding belly, there were no signs that you were there at all. No wiggling, no kicking, nothing. Mrs. Wilson could hear your heartbeat and she was quite satisfied that you were inside; but up until about the fifth month, you were a very still baby. For a few weeks you tossed and turned. I remember Katie and I would sometimes watch Juliana's belly twist from side to side as you flipped around. After about the sixth month everything got too tight and you didn't move very much."

"How was Katie with all of this?"

I chuckled, "She was four and it wasn't about her. The process was far too slow to be of much interest to your sister at the time." I stroked the cat's head for a moment, "Unfortunately the pregnancy was especially hard on Juliana."

"Aren't pregnancies all pretty much the same?"

I smiled and shook my head, "No, they're all different. Juliana was small and very young; remember she was only fourteen at the time, not even really an adult. Mrs. Wilson thought that those two things were causing all sorts of difficulties for her."

I wriggled my nose for emphasis, "The most distressing problem was the vomiting. Just like a silent little Church mouse, nearly every morning she'd secretly endure the most extreme and drawn out bouts of morning sickness. Long before I'd get up I would hear her barfing in the bathroom. Even Katie mentioned it a few times. Later in the day when everything had returned to normal, Juliana wouldn't even admit that it had happened."

Renita was horrified.

"She ate a lot of dry toast for several months which seemed to settle her stomach. Other than the terrible morning sickness and some minor tenderness here and there, everything *seemed* to be OK. During one of the frequent checkups that Mrs. Wilson did at our house we stumbled onto several other problems that had been especially troubling for Juliana. "

"Mrs. Wilson called her friend in Tucson to act as a translator. For a few minutes the two midwives talked, Mrs. Wilson told her friend about Juliana's health and asked her to relay the results to the mother-to-be. I remember she added, 'Ask her if she has any concerns about her health and having a baby.' Strangely that was all that it took to discover Juliana's well hidden anguish."

I'm here to help

With a fascinating look of empathy towards someone whom she'd never known, Renita beckoned me to continue.

"They talked nonstop in Spanish for nearly thirty minutes. Near the end of the conversation, Juliana's eyes were misty and she just nodded and answered 'OK.' She handed the phone to me and Mrs. Wilson led her away to the kitchen."

"What took so long to work out?"

"Juliana had said that she was very grateful that we were taking care of her and felt she could never repay us. I knew that she was afraid of doctors but she insisted that she would not have the baby at a hospital or even venture into a doctor's office or clinic. In retrospect, I think it might have had something to do with her feeling guilty about me supposedly spending so much money to take care of her."

Renita tipped her head, "Was it expensive?"

"You were worth it." I kissed her forehead. "No, not really expensive; remember after Jack's death and all of the insurance payoffs and death benefits, I had plenty of money."

Finally Renita smiled a bit.

"Even though I'd had Katie at home, I certainly visited the OB/GYN during my pregnancy. I

64

wasn't at all happy that Juliana had refused to be checked over by a doctor. Mrs. Wilson told me not to worry, she would 'personally ship Juliana off to the Emergency Room' should any life threatening problems arise."

I scowled as I remembered the more vexing problems, "The translator told me that Juliana also seemed terribly despondent and isolated. She felt *so* guilty about so many things that she'd done."

"Like what?"

"The list was long and daunting: She'd run away from home, gotten pregnant without getting married, she'd apparently stolen some money and food at some point, she'd tricked at least us into thinking that she worked at the hotel, she broke into our car to hide in the trunk, she snuck across the border. I think there was more, but that's all that I can remember."

"None of those things seem so bad." Renita frowned as she considered her mother's motivations. "She was really young, poor and had been abused; somehow she'd gotten pregnant, maybe unwillingly, and she just wanted what was best for her baby."

"Yeah; I realized the same things, but I'm afraid that Juliana didn't, she was even worried that she was eating our food without paying for her fair share."

14

Renita frowned, "Did you have to call the woman in Tucson every time you wanted to communicate with Juliana?"

"No," I chuckled, "after two or three months we developed an imperfect 'family language,' I guess that you'd call it 'Spanglish' now. Often Katie was the intermediary between Juliana and me for tricky or complex conversations. Your sister had learned a surprising amount of Spanish, or at least a very simple version of it, by being around Juliana all of the time."

Renita rolled her eyes, "Maybe that's why she did so well in high school Spanish."

"I guess you're right. She certainly did much better than you did," I pointed out.
"Unfortunately there were several subjects that I didn't want a four-year-old involved in, like problems with adult anatomy or questions about Juliana's murky past. Katie was also especially unwilling to talk to Juliana about Jack."

"Why?"

"I'm not really sure, she still won't say much about him. I think that when she was little she could only cope with her daddy's sudden death by moving on and ignoring the past."

Renita frowned, "I would have loved to have known Jack or my real dad for that matter."

"Several times after Jack died, the Firefighter's Union Rep stopped by to explain all of the paperwork for settling the estate. I always had him visit in the afternoon while Katie was napping, mainly so that she would stay out of trouble but also not to reminded her of her daddy's death. I do recall that Juliana was also rather leery of the Union guy."

"Mmm," I tapped my chin with a sudden realization, "we nearly always talked about money and I'd end up signing a big stack of papers. I wonder if Juliana thought that he was a bill collector?"

"Maybe," Renita nodded.

"That would certainly explain why she was so worried about not paying for her fair share."

I scanned the wall for another photo. "Ah, I'd almost forgotten about that." I retrieved a small brown wooden frame and handed it to Renita. "Not only was I settling Jack's estate and helping out with Juliana's pregnancy but I was also hunting around for a preschool for your sister."

"She went to 'Kinder Cats' like I did, right?"

I'm here to help

"Yep, but there are at least ten preschools within walking distance and with this being the first time that I'd had anything to do with the schools in the area, I decided to check them all."

Renita shook her head, "This picture wasn't taken at Kinder Cats."

In the photo, Katie stood atop an elaborate play structure castle with a wide grin and a colorful cardboard crown.

"She really liked it there. That's 'Royal Care' on Claremont Street. Being the super picky first timer that I was then, I crossed it off the list because there were almost no boys at the school."

Renita laughed, "So Royal Care was really only for princesses in training?"

"I guess so," I returned the frame to the wall. "Juliana came along on some of the visits, especially if we went just before lunch time when the chance of morning sickness was diminished. She was surprisingly shy and self-conscious at the schools. I remember one overly friendly teacher patting Juliana's big belly and teasing her about getting a jump on picking out a preschool. She was mortified."

"That's kind of creepy."

"It strange how often people ignore social restrictions on fondling when women are pregnant."

"I've definitely seen that happen before," Renita frowned.

"Although we hadn't ever really talked about it, I had always imagined that Juliana and her baby would stay, if not at our house, then nearby. I set about rearranging the spare bedroom, which is your room now, to be used as a nursery for the baby and possibly, before the birth, as a separate bedroom for Juliana."

"Wait a minute, I'm confused," Renita tipped her head, "where was Juliana sleeping?"

"She and Katie were still crammed into your sister's little bed."

"That couldn't have been very comfortable, when we were kids I remember sharing a bed with Katie once in awhile. She's a noisy sleeper and she kicks a lot."

I shrugged, "Juliana didn't mind. Putting together the nursery was one of those projects that no one seemed to want but I did anyway. I painted the whole room eggshell white. I went out and bought that cute Queen Anne crib that was in your room for so many years after you moved into the regular bed. I put in a lovely wallpaper border with the storks and baby rattles. It was so adorable."

"What did Juliana and Katie think of it?"

I sighed, "Neither of them liked it. Katie was upset that she was apparently going to lose her bunkmate. Juliana didn't seem to want to sleep alone. Eventually I coaxed her into using the room a few times. When I'd check on her just before I'd go to bed myself, she would be sound asleep on the big bed in the nursery. But then I'd find out later from Katie that Juliana was back in her bed in the morning. Finally I just gave up and let her sleep where ever she wanted."

"You do this all the time," Renita scowled, "I know you think it was helpful and well-meaning, but you were trying to impose your will on Katie and Juliana by insisting on them sleeping separately."

"But I..."

"NO! You didn't ask them and they didn't want it!" Renita fumed. "You thought that if you made a big enough deal about it that they would fall in line and do it your way."

I recoiled from the scolding. I knew she was right; I'd often done the same things to her.

15

We sat together on the sofa in an indignant silence.

I glanced sideways, Renita was still furious about my tendency to be overbearing and I certainly was still irritated that she'd brought it up.

Perhaps we'd unwittingly come to the end of the saga without reaching the conclusion.

In the temperamental world of teenagers unexpected flares of rage and treachery or adoration and awe are common. The young are still bound to see the full extent of both the excitement and the horror of the world around them. Adults protect themselves from the continuous and unpredictable battering by compressing it all down to a manageable median. Ever flattening the highs and lows of life to eliminate surprises. Eventually nothing is particularly painful to bear at the expense of any fleeting exhilaration being reduced to merely a brief grin of mild amusement.

My own distaste at hearing others point out my obvious faults threatened to deprive Renita of finally learning the truth about her past; truth that no one knew but me.

I'm here to help

I sighed. "You're right, I'm sorry that I'm too pushy sometimes."

Renita glared angrily at me.

"I'll try to avoid forcing my ideas onto others."

Her eyes narrowed as she considered my apology, "Will you back off if I tell you that I don't want to do something your way?"

I nodded tepidly, "I'll try."

Renita's expression eased a bit, "Maybe I can eventually get Katie to do the same thing."

I turned to her and smiled, "Maybe."

The acrimonious stalemate had been broken.

For several seconds I forced my attention back to the events that had led up to Renita's birth. There were certainly many emotional ups and downs then as well.

"You may recall doing this just before you started preschool; at Kinder Cats prospective students visit the school several times for the morning session."

"On Wednesdays, I remember that a lot of kids didn't handle it very well," she nodded. "How did Katie do? Was she all clingy and weepy?"

"Surprisingly she was just fine. Juliana was not. The first few days that Katie was out of the house for the morning, Juliana paced around with nothing to do. She would fidget with your sister's toys, straightening the already tidy collection. I recall watching her refold several of Katie's shirts and fiddle about with the shoelaces on a pair of spare tennis shoes. I really hadn't realized how important tending to Katie was for Juliana."

"Well, that was pretty much all that she'd done since she knocked on the door at the resort in Mexico, right?"

"I suppose so," I mentally reviewed the daily routine that had quickly developed when Juliana had become part of our household. "Suddenly, at least for several hours every Wednesday morning, Juliana had no real purpose in life. I suspect that the lurking demons from her past made themselves abundantly obvious to her without the constant clamoring of your demanding sister to drown them out."

Renita fretted over the fragile mental state of the mother she'd never known.

She bit her lip, "Well, you said she felt guilty about her past but we know there were problems with abusive relatives, all of the difficulties of being a runaway teenage girl and who knows what happened to her that led to the pregnancy."

I'm here to help

"Perhaps also abandonment," I suggested, "that certainly could have been the sordid end result of whatever it was that led to Juliana's pregnancy."

Renita's shoulders slumped, "I have this awful feeling that I was probably an unwanted love child."

I cringed at her likely accurate assertion.

16

As I watched her sulk over the grim reckoning of the events that had transpired long ago over which she'd had no control, I was suddenly struck by how much Renita really reminded me of her mother. I'd occasionally seen Juliana ponder some deep and troubling issue, her face a dark silent mask of despair, only to quickly revert to a more neutral demeanor when she'd noticed my gawking.

I would certainly have to forewarn her of the terrible consequences of unaddressed clinical depression.

"Things were finally falling into place," I declared, trying to lighten the mood. "I'd gotten your sister into Kinder Cats and Juliana was more or less over her terrible bouts of morning sickness. Your mom was so small to begin with, her midsection seemed especially gigantic to me just before you were born but she certainly never complained about it. I finally settled Jack's estate and had gotten a considerable life insurance payoff."

Renita tipped her head, "Is that why you never had to work?"

I'm here to help

I nodded smugly, "The money's likely to last until I'm fifty-five and then I can start collecting on his retirement plan."

"When I was in Third Grade, kids didn't believe me when I told them that no one at our house worked."

"I sometimes feel that it is a paltry compensation for losing Jack." Now I felt gloomy again. I forced a smile; "Let me see if I can find something a little more upbeat."

"Please," Renita looked spent from the hours of highs and lows.

"Here's a nice one," I stood and selected a snapshot that I'd taken with a tripod and the windup auto timer on my old camera. Katie, Juliana and I were formally attired and seated at our kitchen table bestrewn with plates and bowls of half consumed delicacies."

"Thanksgiving?" Renita guessed.

"Yes, it was a subdued affair that year. Aunt Deloris had invited us to her house but without Jack around and with Juliana being eight months pregnant, I just didn't want to be part of a big noisy undertaking."

Renita studied the photo, "So what did you guys do?"

"We had a quiet little meal here. I had everyone dress up and I cooked a *really* small turkey. It was particularly amusing because Juliana thought that our undersized bird was a big chicken. She'd never had turkey before and she decided that she liked it."

I laughed, "During dinner Katie kept building tiny alpine dioramas on her dinner plate with mashed potatoes, gravy, steamed broccoli and asparagus. Even though she was misbehaving terribly, both Juliana and I enjoyed her kooky creativity with her food."

"We had cherry pie for dessert. Afterwards Katie and Juliana sang a Spanish tune about feasts."

"How did the song go?" Renita wondered.

"I've forgotten how it went but Katie might remember it if you ask her."

Renita shrugged, "I was just wondering. Sometimes she sang to me in Spanish when I was really little."

"Yeah, I remember that too," I smiled. "About halfway through December I got a call from Mrs. Wilson. It was about at the earliest likely point when Juliana might go into labor, although firstborns are nearly always late. Our old midwife was bedridden with a nasty case of the flu."

I'm here to help

"But she did deliver me, right?"

"Fortunately yes. When I asked her what I should do if Juliana went into labor before she recovered, Mrs. Wilson groaned, 'Well Sharon, you'll have to send her to the hospital.' When I told Juliana about that she had a terrible panic attack. I recall that she locked herself in the bathroom for most of the afternoon. I remember taking Katie out into the backyard a couple of times to pee into an old terra cotta flower pot."

"Oh my god, that's so funny!" Renita chortled, "Katie hates that kind of thing."

"Yes she does," I nodded knowingly. "Mrs. Wilson was feeling much better a few days later."

17

"Christmas came and went; it was my first in twelve years without Jack and the one and only Christmas that we spent with Juliana."

I couldn't stop grinning as I recalled the giddiness and excitement that I'd felt just before Renita was born. "Mrs. Wilson had estimated that you would arrive between Christmas and New Years Day. I personally hoped for the 28th of December because it was right in the middle between the two; you wouldn't have to share the spotlight with all of the shenanigans of either holiday."

"Well, December 27th," Renita laughed, "you were pretty close."

"I scurried around the house on the day after Christmas with Katie and a very pregnant Juliana straightening up after the holiday and doing the final setup for the birth."

"What exactly has to happen when a baby is born at home?"

"It's so much easier if you've done it before," I chuckled, "and if you're not the one giving birth. Mainly you need a clean quiet room and lots of towels that you're willing to toss out afterwards. I put a plastic mattress cover on the bed in your room but no sheets."

"I was born in my room?" Renita interrupted. "I didn't know that." She thought about the revelation for several seconds. "Because I've always known that I was adopted I assumed that I was born in a hospital somewhere."

"Does it make a difference?"

"No," she answered slowly, "I guess I'll just have to mentally change what I imagined about the past."

"Finally around lunchtime the house was more or less cleaned up. Juliana was exhausted, the poor thing." I studied Renita and considered how to help her understand about the ordeal that her pregnant mother went through so many years ago. "Stand up for a minute, sweetie."

Renita shrugged and complied.

As dainty and slimly-built as she was, Renita was a good six inches taller than Juliana.

"Your mom was much smaller than you and nearly four years younger. Try to remember yourself as a fourteen-year-old."

Renita tilted her head and stared off. "I was such a clueless little dweeb. I was just starting High School and I was *so* awkward."
80

"But you weren't nine months pregnant."

She struggled to visualize herself as an expectant teenager.

"If we strapped three or four stiff pillows around your waist and added forty pounds of extra weight, perhaps had you barf several times a day and put you into a town where no one spoke your language, that's what it was like for Juliana just before you were born."

Renita grimaced, "Why would anyone want to have a baby?"

"Pregnancy is tough but it's not all bad; when it's over, you have a darling little newborn to cuddle and love."

For several seconds she stared at her trim abdomen before sitting next to me on the sofa. "Where was Katie when I was born?"

"The day before I drove her over to Aunt Deloris's house. Although I'm sure she knew that Juliana was going to give birth sometime soon, she really had no idea of what that meant. During the trip I told her that she'd stay with Aunt Deloris for about a week and when she came back home there would be a baby in the house."

"What did she say to that?" Renita smirked.

"She could have care less. I was quite annoyed with her because she was much more interested in the litter of six week old kittens that your Aunt had than she was in the impending arrival of an infant at our house."

"I got back home at about dinnertime. Even in her overburdened state, Juliana had a very nice dinner waiting for me. For half a day the house was absurdly quiet without your rambunctious sister."

"The next morning at about eight, I noticed Juliana stop as she was walking around in the kitchen. She held on to the edge of the table with one hand and her belly with the other hand. I asked her if she was OK. She shook her head and said, 'No Sharon. Niño come out now.' I called Mrs. Wilson and she arrived at about nine-thirty."

"What took her so long?" Renita frowned.

I laughed, "It was fine, dear. There was no big hurry, the process of labor takes forever with first-time moms."

"Juliana was definitely having contractions when Mrs. Wilson knocked on the door. She carried in two or three medical bags of supplies and equipment and led Juliana into the room that we'd prepared earlier. The old midwife spent several minutes checking over the mom-to-be. My job in the whole matter was to help

82

out as much as possible without getting in the way."

"Part way through the long labor, I remember being struck by the startling contrast between the two of them. Mrs. Wilson was slow, methodical and more than a little work-weary. She was a plump seventy-year-old with thinning white hair. Juliana was a lightly-built teenager, wide-eyed and wary, frightened and edgy to the point of being almost herky-jerky."

"How did it go?"

I smiled, "I wouldn't say that it was easy because I don't think any birth really is, but it was surprisingly uneventful. Fortunately for Juliana, you had done your part to help out."

"Really?" Renita wondered, "What did I do?"

"You were small and thin." I leaned over and kissed her forehead, "You finally arrived at 7:02 PM."

18

I smiled adoringly at her, "Oh, you were *so* precious when you were born. Six pounds and two ounces with huge dark eyes, smooth brown skin and little wisps of dark wavy hair, you were one of the most beautiful newborns that I've ever seen."

Renita relished the gushing praise. "How was Juliana right after the birth?"

"Tired and relieved." I thought about what was most certainly the high point of my brief relationship with the young woman. "Often, right after a birth, a new mother has a soaring feeling of elation. I suspect it has something to do with hormones being rejigged. For a few hours, Juliana was very happy and quite confident."

I retrieved a photo from the wall and handed it to Renita, "This is the first picture of you."

Although she certainly had seen the photograph many times in the past and perhaps even knew of its importance as the first image of herself, Renita spent many minutes carefully studying the old print.

"You were two days old, it was the middle of a warm and sunny afternoon. Juliana was napping and you were a bit fussy so I carried you around the house for several hours as I straightened up. It was the first time that I had you all to myself. Eventually I snapped this picture."

Renita looked up and smiled, "So I had two moms when I was a baby?"

"I guess three, if you count Katie."

"I had *such* big eyes," Renita lingered over the image.

"Mrs. Wilson was satisfied that both you and Juliana were in good health just after the birth. She tended to Juliana and I gently cleaned you up and wrapped you in several blankets. Mrs. Wilson spent a good forty-five minutes instructing Juliana as to how to breast-feed you."

"How did that go?" Renita handed the frame back to me.

I chuckled, "Juliana was much better at it than you, I'm afraid to say. She apparently had carefully watched someone in the past as they fed a baby and knew exactly what to do."

"You on the other hand," I shook my head mockingly, "kept falling asleep or getting distracted by Mrs. Wilson's voice. Eventually we decided that you would eat when you were hungry."

I'm here to help

"As a birthday present to you and Juliana, I paid off Mrs. Wilson and she produced the application for the Birth Certificate." I stopped suddenly to consider how much I should tell Renita about what had transpired next; my often quite judgmental daughter might well reduce the many moral shades of gray down to a stark and unforgiving black and white of right or wrong.

My long vacillation apparently tipped Renita off to the conundrum.

"What?" she prompted.

"Things got a little strange when Juliana saw the official paperwork. She very carefully examined the application. I remember watching her lips move as she painstakingly deciphered each line and mentally translated it into Spanish. She pointed to one line and asked, '¿qué es esto?' what is this?"

Renita's attention was keenly drawn to the mention of the Birth Certificate that had been the source of her own distress much earlier in the day.

"Mrs. Wilson looked over Juliana's shoulder and read the line out loud, 'Witness to Live Birth.' We both tried to recall what the Spanish translation for 'Witness' was, finally Mrs. Wilson smiled and said, 'Testigo.' She recalled that a Spanish witness goes to court to testify; so testi...go."

Renita laughed, "That's a funny way to remember it."

"Juliana was especially concerned about that line on the application. I remember that she tapped at the space where the Witness would sign and said sternly, 'Juliana.' Mrs. Wilson shook her head and pointed at the line for the Mother of Newborn."

"Juliana was quite emphatic about how the form should be completed. 'NO!' she said, '*Sharon es la madre de la niña. Juliana es la testiga.*' Her harsh expression left no room for compromise."

"She wanted you to be listed as my mom," Renita reiterated, "and she should be listed as the witness? Why do it that way?"

"I was particularly confused but Mrs. Wilson had been through this sort of thing before; she said that occasionally very young and unwed Hispanic women who had crossed the border alone without papers had done similar things to assure the well-being of their babies should the women be suddenly deported."

"So the baby would stay with the 'fake' mother because officially she was the 'real' mom?"

"The three of us fiddled around with the form off and on for a few hours as Mrs. Wilson tidied up. Juliana was absolutely insistent that I should

87

be listed as your mother. Mrs. Wilson was fairly indifferent, officially she was required to uphold the law and list Juliana as your mom but she'd been party to similar chicanery in the past. As long as she could plausibly deny knowledge of the misdeed in the future should something go wrong, she would go along with Juliana's wishes."

Renita was now caught in the moral dilemma that had ensnared me many years earlier.

"I wasn't quite sure of what to do, I understood that Juliana wanted some sort of guaranteed security for you should anything happen to her, but I was also quite reluctant to commit myself to such a vague and formidable future responsibility."

Renita's sour expression continued.

"Finally late in the evening Mrs. Wilson gathered up her things and said goodbye."

"What about the application?" Renita wondered.

"She signed the blank copy and winked at me, 'If you'd fill out the rest of the form to your satisfaction and file it at the County Records Office in the next few days, that would really help me out, Sharon.' I took that to mean that if names ended up on the wrong lines, we could all feign ignorance."

"Three or four days later, on my way to Aunt Deloris's house to pick up Katie, I stopped by the County Offices. On a whim I added Jack's name as your father while I waited in line. When it was my turn, I silently handed the erroneous application and the twelve dollar filing fee to the County Clerk and the deed was done. We got your Official Certificate of Live Birth about six weeks later."

"You broke the law?" Renita was unnerved by the illicit implications of what I'd done.

"Yep," I nodded. "It was cocky and self-serving but at the time that you were born many people had misgivings about government meddling and regulations."

Renita scowled.

I gestured to the right; "The Harlow's next door secretly added a two room addition to the back of their house one summer. Mr. Chin across the street grew pot and peyote in his backyard for years. Those two college boys who rented the corner house ran an auto repair shop in their garage. Some transposed information on a birth certificate seemed a rather minor transgression compared to the rampant felonious endeavors of our neighbors."

Renita ruminated over the deceit.

19

While Renita brooded over the minor-league conspiracy that had produced her fraudulent Birth Certificate, I searched around for several photos that seemed to capture the mood of our household in the weeks after she was born.

"Unfortunately the happy times for Juliana didn't last." I handed her the first frame.

Renita examined the somber image. Juliana stood dolefully at the doorway to the kitchen, the darkened hallway stretched out behind her. Her expression was equally dark. She wearily held the sleeping baby.

Renita glanced up at me with concern, "What was wrong with her in this picture?"

"It was late at night, maybe a week or two after you were born. Just before I was about to go to bed at around midnight, Juliana brought you into the kitchen. I happened to snap the picture just as she walked in."

"Was I fussy or something?"

"No," I whispered. I now recalled how poignant the moments had been just after the image was recorded.

"What was the problem then?"

"She handed you to me in despair and said, *'Sharon, té crías Renita.'* I guessed at the time that she wanted me to look after you so that she could sleep through the night."

Renita studied the picture, "Well she does look really tired."

"Every language has its subtleties and double meanings." I paused to consider if I should continue with my interpretation of the incident. "Her dispirited tone caused me to remember the phrase. Later I repeated it to the translator."

"What does it mean?"

"As I'd assumed, it comes out as 'Sharon, you feed or nurse Renita,' but much more troubling it can also mean 'Sharon, you *raise* Renita.' One way it's an innocent request, the other is much more sinister."

Renita's eyes grew huge as she considered the episode, "What happened after that?"

"I took you to bed with me. You woke up a few times. I fed you and changed your diaper. I could nearly do it in my sleep, I'd been through the same thing hundreds of time before when Katie was a newborn. The next morning Juliana seemed a bit better."

I'm here to help

Renita was still unnerved by the story that the photo had elicited. She handed the frame back to me.

I peered at the other images and selected the most innocent one, "For a few weeks, before the novelty wore off, Katie took an interest in you." I handed her the first photograph.

"Oh, this is so cute!"

In the snapshot, Katie was sitting in the middle of an overstuffed playpen next to the ever-so-tiny baby Renita. Both gleeful girls were completely surrounded by the dozen or so teddy bears that Katie had carried one by one from her bedroom to deposit around Renita.

I held up another picture, "For the life of me, I can't remember who took this one but it's my favorite of us together." It was a close up of me as I held Renita just in front of my face. My lips were puckered and poised just over her tiny forehead. Undoubtedly seconds later I'd kissed her.

Renita smiled, "That one is adorable too."

"Here's another one with you and Katie."

With proud big kid smile, Katie held a bottle a bit askew but nonetheless effectively as she sat on the sofa feeding Renita.

I gawked over Renita's shoulder as she scrutinized the snapshot. "Your sister hounded Juliana and me for days to get a chance to feed you. Sadly the novelty of having you around wore off just after this picture was taken."

"I'm not too surprised."

"Katie started acting up, I'm sure she was resentful about not being the center of attention. Both of the adults in the house were spending most of their time tending to the newborn. Although she was certainly crabby with me, she became especially spiteful towards Juliana."

I winced as I recalled the emotional havoc that she had wrought. "Katie seemed to think that Juliana had abandoned her. She didn't sleep in Katie's bed anymore, she was often too tired to play with your sister and, rightly so, she was preoccupied with her own child. Katie told Juliana several times that she didn't like her anymore."

"What a little brat!"

"She really was, I'm afraid to say. None of this was good for Juliana. After a few weeks of what I considered the normal blues that follow having a baby, Juliana seemed to be getting progressively more depressed. Fortunately Katie started preschool a few weeks after you were born and Juliana and I got a short daily break from the vindictive little green-eyed monster."

"Did you try to help Juliana out of the blues?"

"I did. When Mrs. Wilson stopped by to check on you two, I spent a good twenty minutes out on the front porch talking to her about it."

Renita cocked her head, "What did she say?"

"Apparently postpartum depression is quite common. I don't think it was as well understood then as it is now. We both guessed that Juliana might also be suffering some lingering self-loathing about being a very young unwed mother as well as suffering through the stigmatism of being an illegal immigrant."

I frowned at the downcast picture of Juliana at the kitchen entryway, "Mrs. Wilson had a remarkably simple routine for helping women to overcome the 'baby blues' that she called The Plan."

"Was it medication or something like that?"

I shook my head, "Only a normal amount of sleep, some sort of light exercise outside in the sun and a return to activities that she enjoyed from before the birth."

"That makes sense, I guess."

20

I'd been ambivalently saving one particular picture for the right moment, glancing at it uneasily several times during the long day of unburdening and confessions; now seemed the time to share the significance of the apparently innocuous image.

I handed the frame to Renita and bit my lip, "This is the last picture that I have of you and Juliana."

She examined the unremarkable snapshot in earnest.

The focus was a bit off and the exposure was bad; had I known how important the moment would prove to be I would have painstaking recorded several more images.

Juliana was seated on the sofa in the living room, ironically the same one that we sat on now, apprehensively holding up two-month-old baby Renita like a floppy and unwilling rag doll. Neither was enjoying the photo opportunity. Katie stood behind the sofa in the shadows pensively watching the ordeal.

"Juliana seems so sad."

I'm here to help

I could feel the energy draining from my body. "She was; she really was. I guess I knew it at the time but I just wasn't quite sure what more I could do about it."

Renita stared up at me in anticipation from the gloomy photograph.

"I called Mrs. Wilson again and told her that Juliana's blues had gotten worse, not better. I remember that the worn-out old midwife sighed in exacerbation on the phone, she'd just spent twenty-seven difficult hours delivering some twins and she was in no mood to deal with my minor concerns about someone else's problems. 'Stick to the plan.' she said wearily. It all sounded so easy."

"So what did you do?"

"Well neither Katie or Mrs. Wilson were much help," I groused. "I still wasn't able to convince your spiteful sister that she should be more forgiving of Juliana's flagging attention. Katie was still particularly indignant about being displaced from the center of Juliana's world. This of course made Juliana even more depressed, on top of all of her other self-perceived failings, her one steadfast friend had abandoned her."

"In retrospect, I should have known better; it was difficult enough for me to deal with the unending demands of a newborn as a well-educated twenty-six-year-old with the help of an attentive husband and the cooing assurances of a well-paid pediatrician. I just can't imagine how hard it was for Juliana as an isolated guilt-ridden fourteen-year-old who didn't speak the language."

"Did anything seem to help to get her out of her funk?"

"Singing, cooking and walking." I grinned a bit. "I struggled to get her to do some of those simple things that she did before the birth. Unfortunately Katie wouldn't sing with her anymore but when she was at preschool, I did manage to coax Juliana into singing a few songs to you."

I dabbed my eyes as I remembered her whispering the sweet Spanish lullabies, "It was *so* precious."

Renita briefly smiled.

"I got out of bed at 6 AM nearly every morning for several weeks to get Juliana up so that she and I could put together breakfast. Many times I just sat at the kitchen table slumberously feeding you a bottle while your mom cooked up toast and eggs for the rest of us."

"So singing and cooking; what was the third thing that you tried?"

I'm here to help

"Walking. I think the walks caused the most visible improvement in Juliana."

"Really?"

"When the weather was good, and that February it was rarely good, I'd insist as an excuse that the baby needed to be outdoors in the sun. The first few times we just stood out on the porch for ten minutes or so. It seemed to make a real difference, Juliana's color was better and she wasn't so glum. Then I realized that you and Juliana could accompany me when I walked to the preschool to pick up Katie at noon everyday. The trip took forever when we first tried it. Juliana could barely drag herself the five blocks and back. Katie was especially annoyed by the slow somber trudge home. I ended up carrying you for most of the way."

"Did it get any better?" Renita wondered.

"Fortunately yes, but not much." I winced as I recalled the protracted daily journeys. "We nearly always had to stop at the busy intersection of Washington and Connecticut near the school so that Juliana could rest for a few minutes. While your mom huffed and puffed and tried to collect herself, I'd carry you around and show you the sights, 'Look Renita! There's an old man walking a dog. Dogs say woof! Oh, see the big truck on the street!' You loved it."

Renita smiled, "I'm sure I did."

As the pleasant little memory gradually slipped away, I knew that it was finally time.

"One morning, about a week and a half after we'd started walking to the preschool, Juliana was waiting at the door with you at 11:15. '¿Sharon, Vamos a Kinder Cats ahora?' she asked. Your mom seemed to really want to walk for the first time. I remember noticing how nicely she'd dressed you up for the occasion. Although it was by no means fast, I recall thinking that she was finally moving along like she had some sort of purpose. Perhaps she was over the worst of the depression."

My voice was shaky and Renita stared at me in dismay.

"We got to Washington and Connecticut and Juliana handed you to me and smiled. She pointed across the street, 'You go, I tie shoe.' She pantomimed making a knot and looked at her feet. I waited until it was safe to cross and dashed through the crosswalk. When I got to the other side, I watched Juliana hunched over fiddling with her shoelaces. Something seemed wrong, it was taking far too long and she kept glancing down the busy thoroughfare."

Renita was frozen in horrified silence.

I'm here to help

"When the County Transit Bus came charging towards the intersection she sprinted towards me. 'No, NO, NO!' I remember screaming."

"It really seemed to happen in slow motion. Juliana dodged and weaved as she ran. I realized that she trying to time it so that the bus would hit her. The horn blared, the brakes shrieked and then Juliana stopped and closed her eyes."

"OH MY GOD! What happened?"

"The bus hit her in the crosswalk. There was a horrible crunching sound," I pressed my hands over my eyes in dread and whispered hoarsely, "it was like a Thanksgiving turkey being smashed to bits with a baseball bat."

"I stood there for several seconds. Smoke from the overheated tires filled the air. People were yelling. The driver and several of the passengers ran out of the bus. I didn't know what had happened to Juliana. Everyone rushed towards the backside of the bus. I heard sirens. Finally someone grabbed my arm, 'Do you know that woman?' They tugged me into the crosswalk just past the front of the bus. She was lying crumpled up in the street. There was blood everywhere. She was barely alive and the ambulance was going to take her away."

"I just stood there clutching you."

I could tell that the long emotional tale was taking a toll on Renita; with a particularly drained and wary look she waited stiffly for me to continue.

"After the ambulance took her away I ran the rest of the way to the preschool. I handed you to one of the startled teachers and told her that a bus had hit Juliana. The owner of Kinder Cats drove me to the hospital and said that they'd look after you and Katie until six."

Oddly, I realized that I hadn't burst into tears as I recounted the tragedy that had nearly claimed the troubled young woman who had given birth to Renita.

"All I could think about as I found my way to the ICU was that she'd made a nearly successful attempt at suicide."

21

"She hung on for an hour or so after I got to the ICU but one by one her vital organs failed."

I dabbed my eyes, "When her heart rhythm started to falter one of the young doctors just shook his head and walked away. I'd never watched anyone die before. With Jack it was over in an instant and I found out about both of my parents deaths hours after they had happened."

Renita wrapped an arm around my shoulder.

"I just stood off to the side in the noisy and chaotic ward while nurses and doctors tended to her with professional detachment. I wasn't supposed to be there, I wasn't a relative. If I made any kind of fuss at all I'm sure they would have sent me out."

In agony I stared at Renita, this was after all, her mother. "I didn't want Juliana to die alone."

Renita squeezed her eyes shut for a moment and took several deep measured breaths. She had done it often as a child when she was faced with intractable difficulties, now I finally understood why. This was how she'd kept herself from crying. "Thank you for looking after her," she whispered.

"At 3:12 in the afternoon, Juliana died."

Renita's shoulders slumped. "I guess for the last couple of hours I knew that's what had happened."

A curious little half smile crept across her face, "Earlier in the day I was sure that you were going to tell me that she left me behind and returned to Mexico. Maybe I'd even be lucky enough to eventually meet her. She'd only be about 32 now."

"I'm afraid not, sweetheart."

After several minutes of brooding over the long-lapsed death, she finally asked, "What happened to her after she died?"

I stood and retrieved a photo from the wall and held the image to my chest, this particular one would only make sense with careful explanation.

"Unlike your sham birth certificate, many stern officials of the hospital and the county would scrutinize her death. Despite Juliana's fear of doctors, she'd died in a hospital. Even though she'd struggled to maintain a safe anonymity, she'd been mortally injured on a public street by a county transit bus. Difficult questions would be asked and reasonable answers would have to be given."

I'm here to help

The forewarning had caused Renita to shift around uncomfortably.

"I decided to provide her with as much dignity as I could without risking too much personal peril. I was now, after all, solely responsible for both you and Katie."

Renita nodded at my preamble.

"In the ICU, the nurses removed the hoses and wires that had enwrapped Juliana like a fine mesh of spider webs. One of the doctors finished up the paperwork and asked me a few questions; standard stuff like name, age and address. I knew it would come up again so I carefully recited some favorably skewed data about your mom. He just jotted down what I'd said."

"A few minutes later, the Pathologist arrived to retrieve her body. Just before he wheeled her away, I stopped him. 'I was her only friend,' I told him, 'who do I contact when I make the final arrangements?' I'm sure the Pathologist answered the same question several times a day. 'The Funeral Home should call this number,' he handed me a business card and left with her remains."

"A police officer was waiting at the Nurse's Station. He asked me to recount the accident. I left out my suspicions about suicide. 'She wasn't paying attention and dashed across the

104

street in a panic. A bus hit her and that was it.'
He scribbled away, writing nearly exactly what
I'd said. 'How did I know the victim? What was
her full name and age? Did I know of any
relatives and where could they be contacted?' I
stuck to the story that I'd told the doctor: She
rented a room from me, I thought her last name
was Gonzales and that she was twenty-three
years old, I knew of no relatives. It was nearly
all lies. Even after she'd died, I was trying to
keep her out of trouble."

"Didn't anyone at the Police Department check
on this stuff?" Renita asked in disbelief.

"There are two or three similar deaths every
month of people with no apparent background
in our county, fortunately nobody paid much
attention to Juliana's."

"Thirty days after she'd passed no one had
claimed her body and she was scheduled for a
pauper's funeral. But I wouldn't let that
happen."

I handed Renita the photograph and she studied
the image.

The two girls in the photo were very young and
dressed formally in their Sunday best. Katie was
nine and Renita was a very shy four-year-old.
I'd very carefully planned this particular
photograph, visiting the site on my own several
times to discern the perfect light and the optimal

angles to convey what I wanted to record. It had paid off, this was the best photo that I'd ever taken. The girls stood solemnly on either side of Jack's headstone, both had nearly perfect little bouquets of yellow roses.

"It was taken on the 5th anniversary of Jack's death."

"I remember this," Renita traced the image for several seconds. "What does this have to do with my mom?"

The intentional subtly of the image could be easily missed.

I tapped on the upper left corner.

Renita held the frame inches from her face and slowly smiled. Two rows back and one to the left in the orderly collection of headstones was an unassuming tan-colored grave marker that simply said, 'Juliana Gonzales - Beloved Mother and Dear Friend.'

She passed the frame back to me, "Thank you."

22

"And so," I drooped after the long saga, "that's how we ended up with each other and why your Birth Certificate is a little sketchy."

Renita ruminated over the strange and tragic tale of her true mother for many minutes. Her face changed several times from brief flashes of rage to gloomy introspection as she considered the months-long events that had transpired more than eighteen years ago.

She scowled, "I've still got a few questions."

"I'd be surprised if you didn't, sweetie."

"Where did my name come from?"

"I don't know. As soon as Juliana knew that you were a girl, she called you Renita. I looked it up once a long time ago, it means 'Rebel' or 'Resistant.' I don't think that you're particularly rebellious but you do have a remarkably strong ability to weather misfortune."

Renita considered my assessment. "Weren't there plenty of people around who know that Juliana was my mom and not you?"

"A few, but not really that many," I tallied up everyone that I could remember, "Certainly

I'm here to help

Mrs. Wilson and Aunt Deloris but they're both
dead now. Some of the older staff at Kinder
Cats but they knew of Juliana's death and I
guess they assumed that I really *had* adopted
you by the time you were a student there. I think
pretty much everyone else including you didn't
question my steadfast assertion for many years
that you were adopted."

She nodded.

"Renita," I stared sternly into her eyes, "I know
now that Juliana suffered from a treatable
mental heath condition, I want you to promise
that you'll tell me if you ever have any bouts of
depression."

"OK," she whispered meekly.

"I lost your mom to clinical depression, I
certainly couldn't bear to lose you too."

After several seconds of somber reflection she
smiled wryly, "I know it sounds strange but did
you end up feeling like Juliana was more like a
little sister than just a friend?"

I thought about her question, "I think I did;
certainly after Jack died and I realized that she
was pregnant. Just as Juliana had done for me
months earlier, when everything went bad for
her, I didn't give up. I tried to help out and
make things right even when it meant breaking
the rules."

108

Renita smiled smugly, "I think Katie would do the same sorts of things for me."

"Please," I implored, "wait until you have a stable adult life before you get pregnant."

She laughed, "OK. What about Juliana's last name? On my Birth Certificate and the headstone it says Juliana Gonzales. Was that really her name?"

"No," I shook my head in dismay. "She signed it that way on your Birth Certificate and I was fairly certain at the time that it was a ruse. After she died, the Coroner's Office couldn't find any records for a Juliana Gonzales in the town where the resort is located."

Renita frowned, "You told the Police that she was twenty-three, would that have made any difference?"

"I don't think so. Gonzales is an especially common name in that part of Mexico, but at the time, Juliana was not. I think they would have stumbled upon any records for a fourteen-year-old named Juliana Gonzales and contacted me with further questions."

"So there's no chance of figuring out anything else about my mom?"

"Well, we do know her true age and first name. Maybe she was from one of the neighboring towns."

Renita gazed off in deep thought for several seconds. She eventually retrieved the fuzzy final picture of Juliana holding her as a two-month-old. "I wonder what my life would have been like if my mom was still around?" she stared intently at the snapshot.

"Well," I chuckled, "you would have gotten better grades in Spanish, I'm sure."

She nodded a bit, "I wonder if she would have taken me back to Mexico or if we would have stayed around here."

"You just can't ever be sure about those sorts of things." I kissed her cheek, "Sometimes late at night when I'm lying awake in bed, I think about how my life would have been different if Jack had lived. We certainly would have had a few more kids. Maybe moved to Montana or something like that."

"But," I smiled, "I also might never have known you."

"I guess that's true." Renita glanced at the photo again, "In a way I ended up being the second kid that you weren't likely to ever have."

"Yeah. After going through that whole long and drawn out tale from beginning to end for the first time, I finally realized that we each lost something that was irreplaceable but also found something that we didn't know that we needed."

She stared at me quizzically.

"I lost the love of my life and the chance to live happily ever after but I found a treasured second daughter."

"I lost a mom but gained a more or less normal childhood," Renita grinned. "What about Juliana?"

"Mmm; in the end she certainly lost her sanity, but for almost a year she did escape the demons that had haunted her from childhood."

"No," Renita shook her head, "there's more than that, I think. Even though she had been mortally wounded by her past, she figured out how to guarantee that her child wouldn't suffer the same fate."

"How?" I wondered.

"She found and followed a promising family back home from Mexico, managed to become part of the household, took care of you and Katie when Jack died, more or less convinced you to file a fake Birth Certificate, made sure that you cared for and adored her out-of-

111

wedlock baby and finally she took herself out of the picture when the guarantee was certain."

"Wow," I considered the nearly flawless string of logic for several seconds, "you could be right."

Renita stared at me for several seconds obviously considering whether to put forth a new thought. "Do you feel like I was an emotional replacement for Dad? I did come along not too long after he died."

I felt surprisingly guilty.

"I suppose that just after you were born I really did wish that you were *my* baby. You were so cute and vulnerable. I certainly missed the warm intimacy that I had with Jack. There really is no other feeling of tenderness and closeness quite like what you feel when you take care of a newborn."

Renita stood and returned the frame to the wall. Her long thin fingers glided over many of the pictures that had been part of the protracted tale.

She stopped and pondered the image that I'd used hours earlier to start the story.

Finally she removed the goofy photo of Jack, Katie and me smiling at the Mexican resort from the wall.

"I just realized that I probably have a few days in August with nothing to do." Renita stared at me with a curious look of determination, "I'd like to visit this resort and get a feeling for the area that is my ancestral home."

I studied my youngest daughter while she lingered over the old snapshot. She had grown into a beautiful young woman and now by all rights she should leave behind the home where she'd spent her youth. "I think that you should."

A twitchy little half smile darted across her face, "Would you come with me, Mom?"

About the book:

Way back on the 26th of November in 2004, during that dreadful time around 2 AM that I had long before dubbed the "Worrying Hour" because I'd often fretted over the difficulties of the day at that dreary time, I sat on the sofa in my Northern California home and wrote out in longhand a treatment for a novel.

I owned a construction company at the time and hadn't done any serious writing since my waning days of college nearly twenty years earlier.

Over several sleepless nights I refined the story and eventually wrote most of the first two chapters. In college, I'd specialized in the writing of short fiction and back then seriously doubted that I could keep up a story long enough to produce a novel length work.

I was quite happy with the sample chapters but other, more pressing matters tugged me away from this first attempt at a novel.

In late March of 2009, as the souring economy put an end to most construction in the San Francisco Bay area, I mentally put together several bits and pieces for an intriguing science fiction novel that I'd been considering for many years. By the beginning of July, I began work on my first novel entitled *Floyd 5.136*. To my great amusement the work was finished about a hundred days later.

As I wrote *Floyd 5.136*, I recalled how much I enjoyed developing a story and crafting it in such a way that it could be shared with others. I resolved to write a dozen novels in five short years.

Since *Floyd 5.136*, which is a tale of human clones from the mid twenty-first century unwittingly trapped in a strange world far in the future, I've completed four other novels. The second work is a gritty urban drama entitled *On the Back of the Beast* about a huge catastrophe that transpires in Northern California. Novel number three is a sequel to *Floyd 5.136* called *Xea in the Library*. The forth manuscript is titled *The Ripple in Space-Time*, a story about an inept group of space pirates, planetary extortion, greedy Warlords and plenty of quantum physics.

The first four books are "big" stories about disasters with plenty of subterfuge and large casts of often-quirky characters.

I decided that the fifth book would be a "small" tale about just two or three ordinary people. I also hoped to work in the idea of a personal history told with several dozen snapshots by the main character. I retrieved the treatment and the sample chapters that I'd written during many sleepless nights more than six years earlier and set about completing *I'm here to help*.

And yes, seven more novels are on the way.

S F Chapman August 31, 2011

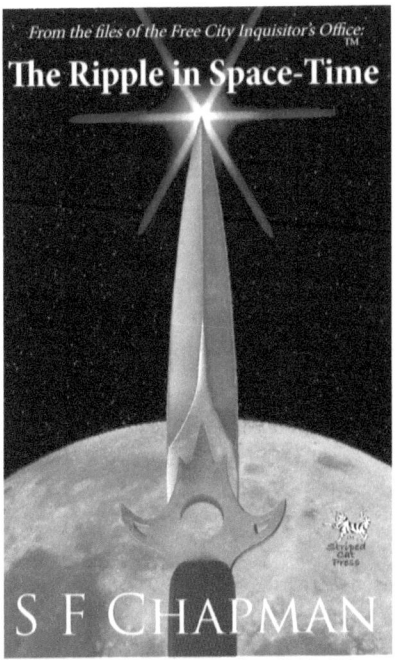

The Ripple in Space-Time by S F Chapman
Available from Striped Cat Press Feb. 2013.

Inspector Ryo Trop of the Free City Inquisitor's Office is called in when the Lunar Ultra Energy Lab is destroyed by a mysterious blast.

Ryo quickly discovers that a complex and sinister scheme is afoot as he searches for clues in the moldering feudal fiefdoms of the Warlords that dominate human affairs in 2445.

As he struggles with the difficult case, the same question keeps popping up: Could the recent wave of space piracy be connected to the disaster?